seriously SILLY stories

The Collection

For Arthur
Who was always there when I needed
him and quite often when I didn't
L·A·

To Laurence
My Seriously Silly friend,
who drove me round the bend
A·R·

Visit the Anholt website at www·anholt·co·uk

ORCHARD BOOKS
96 Leonard Street, London EC2A 4XD
Orchard Books Australia
32/45-51 Huntley Street, Alexandria, NSW 2015
ISBN 1 84121 037 4
This collection first published
in Great Britain in 1999 by Orchard Books
Text © Laurence Anholt 1999
Illustrations © Arthur Robins 1999
The rights of Laurence Anholt to be identified as the author
and Arthur Robins as the illustrator of this work
have been asserted by them in accordance with the
Copyright, Designs and Patents Act, 1988.
A CIP catalogue record for this book
is available from the British Library.
4 6 8 10 9 7 5 3
Printed in Hong Kong/ China

seriously SILLY stories
The Collection

More stories than
you can count
on the fingers
of three feet!

Laurence Anholt ☆ Arthur Robins

ORCHARD BOOKS

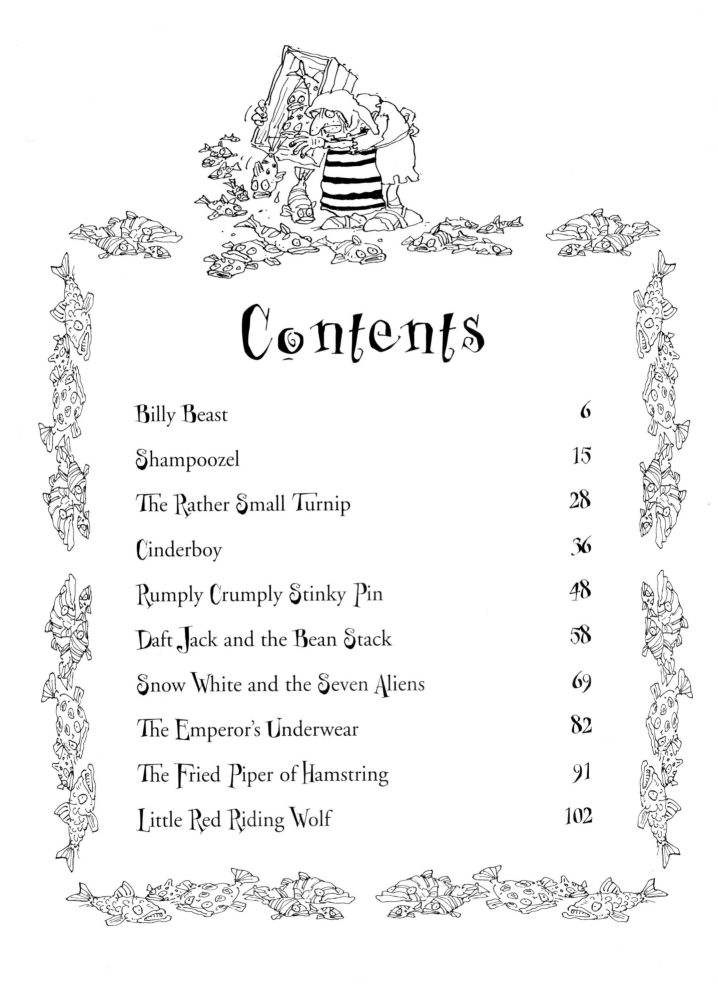

Contents

There was a sad and grumpy King
Who said, "I'm bored as anything,
I'd share my kingdom half and half
With someone who could make me laugh."

Forward stepped a tiny Fool.
He said, "Hey King, that's really cool,
The tales I tell are SERIOUSLY SILLY,
You'll laugh your head off, willy-nilly."

Billy Beast

The King just yawned and picked a nail.
"I'll chop YOUR head off if you fail."
The Fool replied, "I'll try at least,
Story One is BILLY BEAST..."

Betty and Benjamin Beast were very proud of their castle.
They thought it was the most wonderful
building for miles around. It had taken them
years to get it just right with lovely green
mouldy walls and black puddles in the corridors.

There were damp, dark bedrooms with snails
on the pillows and smelly cellars too.

At weekends, you would always find Benjamin
up a stepladder whistling happily as he hung
new cobwebs in corners or painted fresh
mud on the ceilings.

And when their beastly
friends came for dinner, it was
hard not to show off the new kitchen
with its sweet little scampering
cockroaches in all the cupboards, and
hot and cold running slime in the taps.

There was only one thing that Betty and Benjamin were more
proud of, and that was their fine young son, Billy Beast.

7

They loved Billy more than words can say and the truth is, Billy was a bit spoiled.

They were always giving him some little treat or other – an enormous pet toad in a box, or as much crunchy earwig ice-cream as a beastly boy could eat, which wasn't very good for him. Billy always had the best of everything – even private belching lessons after Beastie School.

By the time he was sixteen Billy had grown into a fine looking beast. He was tall and strong with plenty of fleas in his hair and the sharpest, brown teeth a beast could wish for.

The truth was, there wasn't a girl beast around who wasn't in love with young Billy, with those twinkling yellow eyes and that cute way he had of wiping his snout with the hairs on the back of his hand – who could resist?

But as far as Benjamin and Betty were concerned, it would have to be a very special girl beast who could be disgusting enough to marry their son.

So the three of them just carried on living happily together from day to day.

Billy and his toad practised their burping and everyone who met the Beast family thought they were the luckiest, smelliest, most horribly beautiful family they had ever met.

Then one morning, Benjamin and Betty went out gathering frogspawn for lunch, leaving young Billy playing quietly with his toad in his bedroom.

Billy heard a noise outside and when he looked out of his window he saw an old man wandering about in their beautiful weedy garden. He had tied his horse to the tree and he was busy STEALING BETTY'S PRIZE WINNING PRICKLY ROSES!

"Hoi! What do you think you're doing?" shouted Billy. "This is a private castle, you know. My mum will eat you if she catches you here."

When the man looked up at the castle and saw young Billy Beast all hairy and horrid with a big toad sitting on his head he was absolutely TERRIFIED.

"Oh p-please don't eat me, Mr Beast," he stammered. "I got lost and…and I promised my beautiful daughter I would bring her a red rose and…"

"Well not from our garden, pal!" snorted Billy.

The man was so frightened, he promised that
he would send his daughter, Beauty,
to marry Billy if he was allowed to go free.

"All right," Billy agreed, "but she'd better
come soon or my dad will be after you too."
"I...I'll send her straight away," said the poor
man, jumping on to his horse.

"And she'd better be as beautiful as
you say," Billy called after him.

"Oh yes, oh yes she is," shouted the man riding away as fast as
he could. "There's nothing in the world more beautiful than my
daughter."

"What? More beautiful than my toad?" called Billy. But the
man was already out of sight.

When Betty and Benjamin came home, Billy told them the
whole story. "I'm going to be married," he
grunted happily, "to the most beautiful girl
in the world – the man said there's nothing
in the world more beautiful than Beauty."

Betty and Benjamin were
very pleased to think of their
son married to the most
beautiful girl in the world,
although they found it hard to believe that
anyone could be quite as good looking as their Billy.

Early next morning, Beauty arrived. Billy saw her horse coming up the hill towards the castle.

He quickly ran to the mirror to make sure his teeth were nice and black and he checked that his breath was good and smelly. He splashed a little skunk juice under his arms – then he ran to the door to meet his bride.

Billy was very excited. As the doorbell rang, he twisted his face into the most beautifully disgusting shape that he could manage, then pulled open the door.

When Beauty saw Billy, she almost fainted on the spot. Billy could understand that, because his handsome looks often made girls feel weak at the knees.

What he couldn't understand was that Beauty wasn't beautiful! In fact she looked just like an ordinary GIRL!

She was hardly hairy at all, except on her head. And her TEETH – they were all sort of white and shiny!

She had a horrid pink NOSE where her snout should be and little FINGERS instead of nice claws. UGH! It was DISGUSTING!

"I bet she hasn't even got a hairy chest," thought Billy in dismay.

Betty and Benjamin were also disappointed, but they tried not to show it.

The poor girl had come a long way to marry their son and she seemed upset too.

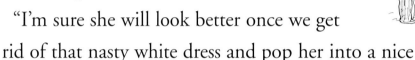

"I'm sure she will look better once we get rid of that nasty white dress and pop her into a nice sloppy mud bath," said Betty kindly.

"And she'll probably get hairier as she gets older," suggested Benjamin. "Perhaps she hasn't been eating a healthy diet – I expect she's hungry now after that long journey. Let's start her off with a lovely bowl of warm earwax and slug juice."

So Betty and Benjamin set about trying to make Beauty a little more beastly, and Billy went into the garden with his toad and sulked.

After a few days, Beauty began to get used to living with the Beasts, and Billy had to admit that she was looking a little better; at least she was getting more smelly.

But then Beauty would go and spoil it all by doing something revolting like washing her hands before a meal or combing her hair and everyone realised that no matter how they tried, Beauty would never be truly disgusting.

Billy promised his parents that he would try to get along with her, although he swore he would never marry her. He patiently taught her to burp nicely and to dribble, but she was slow to learn.

Then, one morning in the garden, something HORRID happened. Billy had just allowed Beauty to play with his toad when she turned around and TRIED TO KISS HIM!

With those white teeth and rosy lips, it almost made poor Billy sick just thinking about it! He wiped his mouth and jumped away.

Beauty began to cry, "I can't help it!" she wailed. "I can't help looking like this. Of course I would like to be hairy and horrid like you. But couldn't you try to love me for what I am instead of the way I look?"

Billy was really a kind-hearted beast. He began to feel sorry for Beauty. He saw that she was right. It doesn't really matter what you look like, it is the person inside that counts.

Before he knew what he was doing, Billy had put down his toad and taken Beauty into his hairy arms, he put his snout close to her little head and…SMACK! He kissed her tiny snubby nose.

BANG. ZAP. WOW!

Right before Billy's yellow eyes, Beauty began to change! She grew hairier and hairier. Her teeth grew brown and longer. Her fingers turned into beautiful claws!

At last she stood before him – a truly wonderful beastie girl with the most gorgeous damp snout Billy had ever seen and a delightful smell of old socks and kangaroo sweat.

Beauty explained that the man who had stolen the roses was not her father, but a wicked wizard who had cast a spell on her.

She would lose her beastly looks until the day someone like Billy was kind enough to kiss her and break the spell.

Billy was so happy, he didn't know what to say. He just dribbled a little. And the beastly couple skipped happily up the steps of the castle, claw in claw, burping excitedly at each other.

And they were all disgustingly happy for the rest of their beastly lives.

The End

Shampoozel

The smallest smile, the faintest grin
Flickered on the royal chin.
The King was feeling most unusual,
Story Two was called SHAMPOOZEL...

There was once a jolly hairdresser named Dan Druff.

Dan LOVED hair!

Curly hair and bristly hair, eyebrows and beards – Dan loved them all. He loved the gleam of his many mirrors and the snippety-snick of sparkling silver scissors.

Dan even sang about hair:

"Hair, hair, glorious hair,
It spreads from your head,
Nearly EVERYWHERE.
It grows on your toes,
Even inside your nose,
Hair, hair, HA-A-A-I-I-R!!"

Only one thing upset Dan's happiness – his girlfriend, Tam O'Tei who lived in the flat upstairs.

Unlike Dan, Tam was a sad person who hid away in her bedroom behind tightly drawn curtains. From under their hairdryers, Dan's customers could hear her wretched moans and Dan nearly tore his hair out with worry over her condition.

The awful truth was…Tam O'Tei had terrible hair!

"Oh, Dan," she wailed. "My head is dull and lifeless. I have a flaky scalp and unsightly split ends, but no ordinary shampoo is effective."

Dan could find nothing to help, and as the days passed, Tam's hair grew as greasy as a chip-shop mop.

Now, not far from the barber shop was an evil black tower which twisted into the sky like a strange hairstyle. This was the home of a Bad Hair Witch.

High in her dark rooms, the Bad Hair Witch mixed strange shampoos and hair-oils which were sold all over the world. The secret ingredients came from rare plants which grew only in her private garden.

Above the hairdresser's shop, Tam became convinced that one of these magical hair herbs would bring life back to her dull scalp and she pleaded with Dan to pick some.

At the mention of the black tower, Dan Druff felt the hairs prickle at the back of his neck. "I dare not go there," he whispered. "What if I should fall into the evil hair-grip of the Bad Hair Witch?"

But Tam O'Tei complained so long and hard, that at last Dan Druff could stand it no longer, "All right, keep your hair on," he bristled. "I will go to the tower and comb the gardens for your herbs."

So the next morning, before dawn, the brave barber crept reluctantly up the hairpin bends that led to the tower.

As he walked, he sang to keep up his courage.

"Hair, hair, MARVELLOUS hair,
The poor can have more,
Than a millionaire.
You may think it sounds silly,
But it grows on my...
w-w-what on earth is that?"

Before he could finish his song,
Dan had almost walked into a huge sign
hanging on the wall before him:

Dan Druff, use your head,
If you climb this wall
You'll wish you were dead.

Dan felt a shiver run along his
moustache. Only the thought of Tam's sad locks drove
him on. Ignoring the sign, he scrambled into the Bad Hair
Witch's secret garden where he found a second sign:

Dan Druff, can't you read?
Don't even think
About nicking a weed.

Poor Dan had never been in such a
hairy situation, but he bent down and
began to stuff his pockets with the herbs.

18

Suddenly he heard a terrible voice:

"Dan Druff, you must be crazy,
You'll pay for those plants
With your very first baby."

Dan's hair stood on end – it was the worst rhyme he had ever heard.

Before him stood…
the Bad Hair Witch!

"B-but I don't have a b-baby," stammered Dan.

"Well let's not split hairs," snapped the witch, "I will wait until your first child is born."

Grabbing a last handful of herbs, Dan leapt over the wall and hared down the hill to the town.

He found Tam in her bedroom wearing a paper bag on her head and he poured out the story of his terrifying brush with the Bad Hair Witch.

But Tam was barely listening. She seized the wonderful herbs, crushed them and began to lather her scalp…

KER-R-POW!!!

As if by magic, Tam's hair turned into a glorious mass of glossy curls which seemed to flow in slow motion when she tossed her head.

19

Tam O'Tei was cured!

She tore downstairs into the sunny shop, and, as Dan shaved the bristly early morning customers, Tam happily set to work beside him, sweeping up the fallen curls and locks.

That very week, Tam and Dan were married and the whole town joined them in this glorious hymn:

Hair, hair, MAGNIFICENT hair,
It can grow down below,
In your underwear.
It grows on your chest,
Like a big woolly nest,
Hair hair HA-A-A-I-I-R!!

Before a year was out, the couple's happiness was complete – a beautiful baby daughter was born, and, after much thought, they called her…SHAMPOOZEL.

In that happy hairy world, not one thought was given to the Bad Hair Witch.

But the Bad Hair Witch had forgotten nothing. High in her tower she worked day and night on her most amazing invention yet – something all barbers dream of – a marvellous, magical HAIR GROWING LOTION!

"Guess which witch will be rich!" she sniggered. "All I need is a helpless, hairless baby to test my invention."

And so the Bad Hair Day dawned. The bell at the little barber shop tinkled cruelly as the Bad Hair Witch burst inside.

"Give me the child!" she shrieked.

"Have you got an appointment?" said Tam. "Let's see, I could fit you in Thursday…"

"You don't understand, you fools. I need to test my new improved formula – Ultimate 2-in-1 Hair Growing Lotion."

"Leave Shampoozel alone," pleaded Tam O'Tei. "You cannot try out your hair-brained inventions on our child."

Ignoring the tears of the unfortunate couple, the Bad Hair Witch seized Shampoozel and carried her back to the tower. To make sure the precious child would never be taken from her, the Hair Witch bricked up the front door behind them.

As the days passed, the Bad Hair Witch grew to love the baby and looked after her as if she were her own.

"No more tears, Baby Shampoozel,
My magic shampoo is very unusual,"
she would sing as she washed the infant's hair.

And day by day, as Shampoozel grew, her hair grew too, in great long golden tresses which tumbled across the floor, down the stairs, into the kitchen, under the dog, round the back of the fridge and back upstairs again. "Hair, hair, HAIR!!" cackled the Bad Hair Witch. "Look at all your beautiful golden hair!"

Sometimes hairy Shampoozel remembered her parents' little barber shop in the town far below. Now that their daughter had gone, Dan and Tam worked sadly and never sang anymore; and so, one by one, the customers went elsewhere.

Years passed, and as Shampoozel grew into a young woman, the Bad Hair Witch taught her the secret art of the hairdresser:

Wash your hair and keep it sweet,
Lather, rinse, repeat.
Rub and comb and keep it neat.
Lather, rinse, repeat.

Together, the Bad Hair Witch and Shampoozel created new hair products which were more amazing that anyone could have dreamed. They became so famous, in fact, that a young prince by the name of Gary Baldie, heard about them from his home in a distant land.

The prince, although handsome and wealthy, was as bald as a billiard ball.

Prince Gary had tried one wig-maker after another but without satisfaction, so when he finally heard about the Ultimate 2-in-1 Hair Growing Lotion, he set out straight away, and after many days arrived at the tower.

Of course even a prince cannot enter a tower without a door. So Prince Gary concealed himself beneath the walls and after a while he saw an amazing thing.

The Bad Hair Witch appeared at the window with her shopping bag. All of a sudden a great mass of hair cascaded to the ground. The witch slid down it and set off towards the town.

"I suppose that's what they call a hair slide!" whispered Prince Gary in amazement.

Half an hour later, the old lady returned with her shopping and called out:

"Shampoozel, Shampoozel,
Let down your hair
So I can climb to the top
Of your long hairy stair."

Shampoozel let down her locks again and the old woman scrambled back up the tower.

Gary Baldie was no fool and the next time the old woman went out, the prince stood below the window himself and called:

"Shampoozel, Shampoozel,
Your hair is so curly,
Let it hang down now,
Be a good girlie."

To his delight, a great coil of hair tumbled to the ground. He seized it and began to baldly go where no man had gone before.

The prince scrambled into Shampoozel's room and when his royal eyes fell on the lovely Shampoozel, he was captivated by her hairiness. He leaned towards her and kissed her ruby red lips.

There and then, Shampoozel and the prince fell in love. Gary told her that he adored her limitless locks, and how he would love to have some of his own. To his amazement, Shampoozel replied that she had grown tired of her hair, "It don't half hurt when people climb up it," she complained. "And, it takes a week to wash."

But then, to the prince's joy, Shampoozel pulled out a tiny bottle of Ultimate 2-in-1 Hair Growing Lotion and began to massage his shiny scalp.

Almost immediately, a single hair popped out of the prince's head. The first hair was followed by a second,

the second by a third, and within ten minutes the prince had a mass of golden curls snaking down his back, nearly as long as Shampoozel's.

Gary Baldie seized Shampoozel and danced with joy.

"My prince, you must wash and go," whispered Shampoozel.

She brushed a few stray hairs from his collar and with one final kiss, the prince climbed down Shampoozel's hair and slipped away into the shadows.

It wasn't long before the Bad Hair Witch returned:

"Shampoozel, Shampoozel,
Don't make me shout,
Let down your hair, girl,
Don't hang about."

As soon as she entered the salon, the witch spotted Gary Baldie's little crown, which Shampoozel had left hanging on the coat hook. The witch was furious and, after a terrible argument, stormed into her bedroom, leaving Shampoozel weeping pitifully.

The prince, meanwhile, had decided that, witch or no witch, he had to see Shampoozel again.

He stood at the foot of the tower and whispered:

"Shampoozel, Shampoozel,
Here is your prince.
Throw down your pigtail,
My hair needs a rinse."

Immediately, a long lock of hair curled out of the window and tumbled to the ground.

But just as the prince was about to climb up, he saw a figure sliding down…it was Shampoozel!

"I don't know why I didn't think of this before," she said. "All that stupid hair. I snipped it off and tied it to the bed. Then I slid down to you. At last we have escaped from the Bad Hair Witch."

"That was a close shave!" replied Gary Baldie, softly stroking her silky stubble. "Come on, let's really let our hair down."

So Shampoozel and her hairy prince ran away to his castle, but she didn't forget her parents, Dan Druff and Tam O'Tei. Although they were rich, Shampoozel and Gary Baldie liked to work in Dan's shop on Saturdays.

Before long, the little barber shop was once again the busiest in the land.

"It's amazing how the customers keep coming back," laughed Dan.

And it was true – some of the customers seemed to have as many as five haircuts a day.

Perhaps they just loved having their hair cut by Shampoozel.

Or perhaps the secret shampoo she uses has something to do with it…her Ultimate 2-in-1 Hair Growing Lotion!

Or perhaps they come for the endless happy songs which drift across the hairy town.

High in her tower, even the Bad Hair Witch joins in:

Hair, hair, SENSATIONAL hair,
Shampoozel's the girl,
To share your hair care.
She can give you a shave,
Or a permanent wa-a-ve,
Hair HAIR...
H-A-A-A-I-I-I-R-R-R!!!!

The End

The Rather Small Turnip

With that the King bit on his knuckles
To try to stop the royal chuckles.
"Another story I recall,
Concerns a TURNIP, rather small..."

Round about lunch time, the greedy farmer began to feel hungry. His huge belly rumbled as he walked across the field.

Suddenly he noticed a rather small turnip…but it was far too small for his lunch.

The farmer called over to his wife.

"Here you are, wife," he said, "you can have this nice turnip for your lunch."

The farmer's wife looked at the rather small turnip. She poked it with her boot.

"You mean old thing!" she said to her husband, "I won't get very fat on that! It's tiny!"

So the farmer's wife called the cow.

29

The cow looked
at the turnip.
She poked it
with her hoof.
"There you are,"
said the farmer and the farmer's
wife, "we're feeling generous
today. You can have this
delicious turnip all for yourself.
Go on, eat it!"

"You must be joking," mooed the cow,
"that's not enough for a big girl like me. Call the goat."

The goat looked at the rather small turnip.

He prodded it with his horn.

"We have chosen this beautiful
turnip especially for
you," said the farmer
and the farmer's wife
and the cow. "Would
you like to eat it here
or take it away?"

"You must be
kidding," bleated the
goat. "I've never seen such a lousy specimen. Give it to the dog."

The dog sniffed the turnip.

"Go on," said the farmer, his wife, the cow and the goat. "It's all yours! Tuck in."

"Don't make me laugh," barked the dog. "I don't even like turnip. Call the cat."

The cat came…slowly.

"Guess what?" said the farmer, the farmer's wife, the cow, the goat and the dog. "It's your lucky day. You can have this turnip boiled, mashed, poached or steamed – all garnished with side salad and served with house wine."

"Humph!" miaowed the cat, looking at the turnip. "I've got bigger blisters than this turnip. Send for the mouse."

The mouse scampered across the field. She came to the place where the farmer, the farmer's wife, the cow, the goat, the dog and the cat were standing. At their feet was the most beautiful turnip she had ever seen.

The mouse stared and her pink nose twitched. She couldn't believe her luck. She LOVED turnips.

She sniffed it. She licked it all over and her eyes sparkled.

"Don't wait for us," said the farmer, the farmer's wife, the cow, the goat, the dog and the cat.

So the tiny mouse began to eat. She nibbled and gnawed.

It took a long time because, to her it was a very BIG turnip.

The others watched and waited and felt more and more hungry. The greedy farmer's belly rumbled.

The mouse crunched…

and scrunched…

And chewed…

…and chomped.

Until, at last, every scrap of the rather small turnip was gone.

Then the tiny mouse burped a tiny burp, sighed a tiny sigh, rubbed her tiny fat mousy tummy… and lay down in the grass for a tiny mousy sleep.

The cat looked at the fat little mouse.

"Now, that's what I call LUNCH!" she growled. And she gobbled up the little mouse in one bite.

Then…the cat was eaten by the dog…

…the dog was eaten by the goat…

…the goat was eaten by the cow…

…the cow was eaten by the farmer's wife…

…and the farmer's wife
was eaten by…

"WAIT A MINUTE!" shouted the
farmer's wife, "You can't eat ME!"

"But what about my lunch," moaned
the greedy farmer. "I'm so hungry!"

"Well," said the farmer's wife patting
her tummy. "You should have eaten
that turnip. IT was absolutely delicious!"

The End

Cinderboy

Then the Fool began this story
About a boy who dreamed of glory.
The grumpy King was seized with joy
To hear about young CINDERBOY...

Cinderboy was crazy about football.

His wicked stepdad and his two lazy stepbrothers were football crazy too. The whole family supported Royal Palace United.

Every Saturday they would lie about on the sofa with the remote control and watch their favourite team on TV. Royal Palace always played brilliantly in their smart pink shorts and shirts.

But not poor Cinderboy. He wasn't even allowed to watch. He had to wait on his stepbrothers hand and foot, and bring them cups of tea and bowl after bowl of peanuts, which were their favourite snack.

Cinderboy's family was very noisy and bad mannered. When Royal Palace scored they would jump up and down on the sofa and shout for more peanuts to celebrate.

And when the other team scored they would throw their peanuts at the TV, then yell at Cinderboy to pick them up so that they could throw them again.

One day his cruel stepfather said to Cinderboy, "Listen, Cinders.

Tomorrow is the day of the big Cup Final. I am taking your stepbrothers to the Royal Palace stadium to watch the match. And while we are gone you must clean the whole house from top to bottom."

"Yes," said his stepbrothers, "we want every last peanut picked up from under the sofa."

Poor Cinderboy was very unhappy. He would have loved to see his team play in the Cup Final more than anything else in the world.

The next morning he had to wake up earlier than ever to prepare peanut butter sandwiches for his horrible brothers who only laughed at the tears in Cinders' eyes.

As they drove away, shouting and tooting the horn, Cinderboy lay on the sofa and cried and cried and cried.

Then he had an idea. He would work as hard as anything and clean the house so that he could watch the big Cup Final on TV.

He set to work straight away

...scrubbing his stepbrothers' smelly football socks

...and hoovering up every last peanut from under the sofa.

When at last the work was done, the house sparkled from top to bottom.

Cinderboy

Cinderboy pulled up his little stool, found the remote control and switched on the TV.

Royal Palace are ma-agic!

Everyone else is tra-agic!

The match had just begun. The terraces were packed with cheering Royal Palace fans. Cinderboy even caught a glimpse of his stepfather and brothers sitting in the front row, waving their pink scarves and throwing peanuts at the referee.

Oh, how Cinderboy wished he could go to a real live football match!

What made him feel even sadder was that Royal Palace were not playing well that day. Soon the other side had scored and Cinderboy felt sadder than ever.

To make matters worse, just before half-time a terrible thing happened – the Royal Palace captain was kicked in the shin and had to be carried off the field on a stretcher.

When the half-time whistle blew, Royal Palace were ten-nil down and struggling without their best player. During the advertisements Cinderboy was crying so hard he could hardly see the television.

Suddenly, a pink face appeared on the TV screen before him.

"Don't cry, Cindy," it said.

Cinderboy rubbed his eyes. There must be something wrong with the television, he thought.

The face seemed to be talking to *him*!

"Who–who–who are you?" he stuttered.

"I am your TV Godmother," said the face on the television. "And guess what, Cindy? You *shall* go to the big Cup Final!"

"But I don't have anything to wear," stammered Cinderboy.

"Don't worry, Cinderboy. Just press button 13 on the remote control," said the TV Godmother.

Cinderboy wiped his eyes with the back of his hand and held out the remote control.

He pressed button 13.

KERBAM!

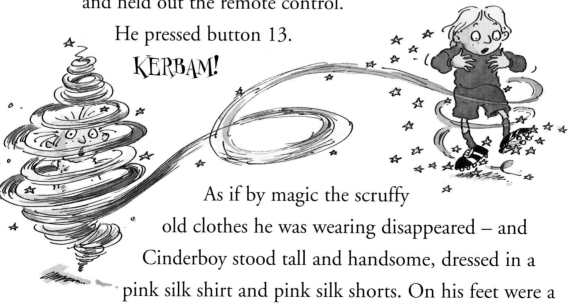

As if by magic the scruffy old clothes he was wearing disappeared – and Cinderboy stood tall and handsome, dressed in a pink silk shirt and pink silk shorts. On his feet were a pair of brand new football boots with gleaming glass studs.

"Oh, thank you, TV Godmother! But…how will I get to the big Cup Final?"

"Oooh, you are the big worrier!" said the voice from the TV. "Press button 14 on the remote control."

Cinderboy pressed button 14.

KERBAM!

As if by magic the old sofa changed into a long shiny pink limousine with a pink uniformed chauffeur at the wheel.

"Oh, thank you! Thank you!" cried Cinderboy.

"Just one thing, Cindy doll," said the face on TV, "no one must recognise you. Wear this mask at all times."

A hand reached out of the screen holding a pink silk mask.

"And most important of all, you must return home before the referee blows the final whistle."

Without a second thought, Cinderboy grabbed the mask and jumped into the limousine and roared out through the door.

It seemed like only seconds before he screeched to a halt in the stadium car park.

Cinderboy pulled on the pink mask and ran towards a big open door. When he looked around, he was standing…

…RIGHT IN THE MIDDLE OF
THE PITCH!

The crowd cheered in excitement as
the mysterious pink-masked player
charged on to the field and headed
straight for the ball. He skilfully tackled
the other players, flicking the ball into the air
with his left foot and sprinting towards the goal post. Then, to
the amazement of the Royal Palace fans – KERBAM! He shot it
into the back of the net!

The man in the mask is MA-AGIC! Everyone else is TRA-AGIC!

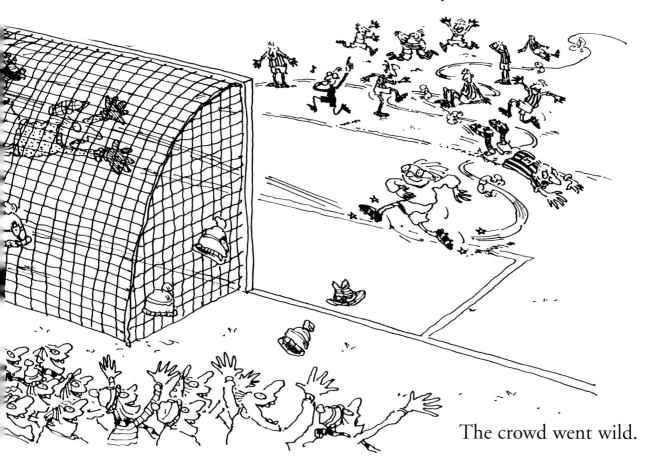

The crowd went wild.

Only ten more minutes to go. Cinderboy manoeuvred the ball around the pitch as gracefully as a dancer at a fairy-tale ball.

Then – KERBOOM! Cinderboy scored again. And – KERBLAM! He headed the ball into the back of the net.

KERWOOMPH! He bounced it into the goal with the tip of his glass-studded boot. The stadium roared with applause.

On a bench at the side of the field the injured Royal Palace captain and Eddy Prince, the team manager, stared in disbelief.

"Whoever that player is," they said, "we *need* him for our team."

Before long, the score was equal – ten all. But soon there were only seconds left to play and the ball was at the wrong end of the field.

Cinderboy noticed the referee put the whistle to his lips.

"TV Godmother, help me!" he whispered.

One last time Cinderboy dived towards the ball. With a mighty swing he kicked it so hard that one of his glass-studded boots flew off and then tumbled to the ground.

The ball shot upwards like a rocket. The whole crowd rose to their feet.

The rival team stood open-mouthed as the ball soared like a bird through the sky. At the other end of the field it began to fall. It bounced once, then dropped effortlessly into the centre of the net. Royal Palace had won the Cup Final! The crowd went ballistic!

A thousand pink caps were thrown into the air.

Eddy Prince raced on to the pitch to sign up the mystery player.

But Cinderboy, remembering the promise to his TV Godmother, ran out of the stadium as fast as his one boot would carry him.

But, to his dismay, when he reached the car park, he found only the battered old sofa where the pink limousine had been.

And poor old Cinderboy had to push the sofa home.

Royal Palace were MAA·AGIC
The rest of the world is TRAA·AGIC

"The man in the pink mask was fantastic. You should have seen him!" shouted the stepbrothers when they finally returned home from the celebrations.

"Yeah!" they smirked, "and poor old Cinderboy missed the whole thing."

Cinderboy only smiled to himself. That night, as he lay in his broken old bed, tears of joy sparkled in his eyes as he dreamed about the day he had scored the winning goal for Royal Palace United, the best team in the whole wide world.

Early the next morning there was a knock at the door. Cinderboy ran to answer it. He couldn't believe his eyes! There stood Eddy Prince, the Royal Palace manager.

"I'm searching for the mysterious boy in the pink mask," he said. "The person who fits this gleaming glass-studded boot will play for the Royal Palace team for the rest of their days."

"Oooh!" said the lazy stepbrothers, coming downstairs in their pyjamas. "Let me try! Let me try! It's no good asking Cinderboy – he didn't even watch the match! Go and fetch some peanuts for Mr Prince, Cinders."

The first greedy stepbrother snatched the glass-studded boot from Eddy Prince.

He tore off his slipper and shoved his sweaty foot into the boot. But no matter how hard he pushed, he couldn't get the boot on.

Then the second greedy stepbrother stepped forward and grabbed the boot.

His foot was slightly smaller and slightly sweatier. He shoved…

and squeezed…

 and pushed…

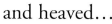 and heaved…

and suddenly – PLOP! His foot was inside.

"IT FITS! IT FITS!" he shouted. "Father, Father, come and look! I'm going to play for Royal Palace!

I'm going to be on telly!

I'm going to be rich!

I'm going to buy a peanut factory…

Everyone's going to cheer, just like

they did for the boy in the pink mask – I mean me, of course."

"Oh!" said Eddy Prince, looking a little surprised. "Are you sure it was you? I'm afraid you'll have to do a little training…"

Suddenly Cinderboy stepped out of the kitchen.

On his face he wore…a pink silk mask!

In his hand was…a tiny pair of pink shorts!

"Well then stepbrother," he said. "Let's see

you fit into these…"

And he held out

the pink shorts.

Everyone gasped. But try as he

might, his stepbrother had eaten too

many peanuts to squeeze into the shorts.

So Cinderboy drove away with Eddy Prince to begin a new life
as Royal Palace's star player.

But being a kind sort of boy, he soon forgave his wicked
stepfather and his greedy brothers and arranged for them to have

as many free tickets as they wanted to

see Royal Palace play.

He even offered to pay for the

operation to have the glass-studded boot

removed from his

stepbrother's foot.

And Cinderboy

lived happily ever after, and scored more

goals for Royal Palace than there are

peanuts under all the sofas in the

whole wide world.

The End

Rumply
Crumply
Stinky Pin

The King was smiling to his ears.
"I haven't felt so good in YEARS!
Come, let another tale begin, of
RUMPLY CRUMPLY STINKY PIN..."

There was once a country where everyone had silly names. They were called 'Mrs Mouse-dropping' or 'Roland Camelbelly', and they called their children 'Little Custardlump' or 'Teeny-Tiny Toenail Clipping'. But the person with the silliest name of all was the King himself and he was very proud of it.

His full title was 'His Royal Niceness Marvin Eggbeard Pyjamadance Birdwhistle Gormangeek Bob-a-job Kneepickle Burp Glub-glub Globba Blobin Eeeeee Woomph Paint-Your-Mother-Green – Junior III'. Which is a pretty good name for a king.

Now, in this country lived a miller by the name of Eyebrow Snailsocks. Eyebrow had a beautiful daughter who he was always boasting about. "Not only is she beautiful," he would say, "but she is clever too. My daughter can do ANYTHING! Why, I bet she could…I bet she could…make string vests out of spaghetti!"

"Don't be silly, Daddy," the girl would say.

And everyone who knew old Eyebrow only laughed.

49

But one day, the King (whose name I have mentioned) heard of Eyebrow's idle boasts.

"Send your daughter to me," he ordered, "let's see how clever she really is."

The miller was very frightened and his daughter began to shake and weep into her apron, but the King's order had to be obeyed.

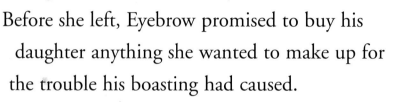

Before she left, Eyebrow promised to buy his daughter anything she wanted to make up for the trouble his boasting had caused.

His daughter couldn't think of anything offhand except perhaps a little fluffy guinea pig for a pet. And this Eyebrow promised her as soon as she returned from the palace (assuming she was still wearing her head).

And so it was that the young girl stood shaking before the King.

"DO YOU KNOW WHO I AM?" he demanded in a deep royal voice.

"Yes sir," whispered the girl. "You are 'His Royal Niceness Marvin Eggbeard Pyjamadance Birdwhistle Gormangeek Bob-a-job Kneepickle Burp Glub-glub Globba Blobin Eeeeee Woomph Paint-Your-Mother-Green – Junior III'."

"Exactly," said the King. "Now, your father has been boasting that you can knit string vests out of spaghetti. I have decided to lock you in a room full of spaghetti and if it isn't all knitted into string vests by sunrise, I will personally tickle your armpits with a wet toothbrush."

Saying this, the King swept out of the room and went off to practise signing his name.

The miller's daughter was in despair, she looked at the mountain of spaghetti and thought of the little fluffy guinea pig she would never see. Then she wept into her apron again.

All of a sudden she heard a funny little laugh. "Tee hee hee hee!"

And looking down at her feet she saw the strangest little man she had ever seen. He wore a pointy hat and had an orange beard which was so long that he had wrapped it three times around his waist.

"Why are you crying, miller's daughter? You're covering the spaghetti in pools of water."

"I know," she sobbed. "I have to knit all this spaghetti into string vests otherwise the King will tickle my armpits with a wet toothbrush."

"Well it just so happens, I'm a spaghetti knitter. There's no one faster and there's no one fitter."

"Oh please help me," sobbed the girl.

The little fellow grabbed an armful of spaghetti and pulled two enormous knitting needles from his pocket. But suddenly, he paused, and looked up at the girl.

"I'll knit your spaghetti at the double
but what will you give me for my trouble?"

The poor girl searched her apron pocket which was soaked with tears and finally pulled out a soggy toffee which the little man seized with delight.

The girl danced with joy as vest after vest flew from the flashing needles.

"Clickety click!
We'll make these vests in a tick."

Early in the morning the King brought the miller to watch the toothbrush tickling.

Of course, he couldn't believe his eyes when he unlocked the door and saw that every last bit of spaghetti had been made into perfect little string vests, all with tomato buttons down the front, as neat as you please.

"What did I tell you?" boasted Eyebrow Snailsocks (pretending not to be surprised). "I said she was clever. My daughter can do ANYTHING! Why I bet…I bet she could make bank notes out of OLD FISH."

"Oh Daddy!" groaned the miller's daughter. But it was too late, the King was already ordering a room to be filled to the ceiling with old fish.

"Right!" he shouted. "If she fails I'll…let's see…I'll plant melon seeds between her toes and…if she succeeds then…I'll marry her."

Well, the miller's daughter didn't much fancy having
melon seeds planted between her toes…
but on the other hand, she didn't like the idea
of being married to the King either;
especially if she was going to be called
'Her Royal Niceness Marvin Eggbeard
Pyjamadance Birdwhistle Gormangeek
Bob-a-job etc.etc'.

As soon as she was alone with the mountain of fish she began to
weep into her apron. Surely no one could make bank notes out
of old fish? Now she was sure she would never have the fluffy
guinea pig her father had promised her.

Suddenly the room was filled with strange laughter…

"Tee hee hee hee! Why are you crying, miller's daughter?
You're covering the fish in pools of water."

…and the little man stood before her again, singing in his
squeaky voice.

The girl told the little man about her father's boasting and the
King's order that she should make bank notes out of old fish.

She was just getting to the bit about the melon seeds, when the
little man pulled a printing press from his pocket and began
throwing the fish in one end and pulling crisp new bank notes
from the other, singing as he worked…

"Haddock, salmon, trout and plaice!
Blow your nose and wipe your face."

"I'll make your bank notes at the double.
What will you give me for my trouble?"

"Anything, anything," promised the poor girl,
frantically searching he apron pockets.
But alas! there was nothing there.

"Miller's daughter you are in my debt,
You must promise me your very first pet."
The girl gladly agreed and by sunrise not
one minnow remained. The room was stacked to the ceiling with
neatly folded, slightly smelly bank notes.

"Let's marry immediately!" shouted the King throwing
open the door.

Eyebrow jumped up and down with delight.
'You see!" he yelled. "I told you she was clever.
This girl can do ANYTHING! Why I bet…I bet…"

But the miller's daughter was gone, down the
stairs and out of the palace.

Later, as he walked home, the miller began to
feel very sorry about all the porky pies he had been
telling, and all the trouble he had caused.

So remembering his promise, he called in
at the pet shop and bought his daughter the
cutest, fluffiest little guinea pig he could find.

The girl was delighted and soon forgot about the

horrid King and the strange little man. But that night as she lay in

her bed listening to her new pet running round and around on his
squeaky wheel, she heard someone laughing outside her door…

"Now don't forget we made a bet,
I've done my work, I want my pet."

The girl didn't wear her apron in bed,
so she wept into her pyjamas instead.

"Don't take my guinea pig," she pleaded.

The little man felt sorry for her and said…

"Okay kid, we'll play a game.
I'll give you two days to guess my name."

In a flash, he was gone. The girl lay awake for the rest of the
night thinking of likely names for him.

The next evening, the little man returned.

"Miller's daughter, I must confess,
If I gave you forever, you still wouldn't guess."

But the plucky girl was determined to try.

"Is it Scrambled Egg Foot?" she asked.

But the little man only laughed…

"Tee hee hee hee!"…and
stroked his long orange beard.

"Is it Plum-Plum-Lemon-Moose Carpet
Ears?" she asked hopefully.

The little man laughed even more.

"Well then, perhaps it's Hubert Crumpet Trumpet-Bum?" the
miller's daughter asked desperately.

"By my long orange beard
My name's much more weird.
Miller's daughter you've got one more day.
But you'll never guess it anyway."

The little man screeched with laughter and in a flash, he was gone, leaving the poor girl more miserable than ever.

The old miller didn't like to see his daughter unhappy, so at breakfast he told her a story to cheer her up.

"I was delivering flour yesterday when I saw the funniest thing; there was a little man wearing a string vest made of spaghetti, dancing outside a tiny caravan and he was singing the most peculiar song."

"Can you remember the song?" asked the girl, her eyes lighting up.

"Well, yes," said her father. He cleared his throat and sang: "I sing and dance a little jig,
  Soon I'll have that guinea pig.
  They can weep a bowl of tears,
  They won't guess my name in a billion years.
It did make me laugh I can tell you!"

"Yes, yes, but didn't he mention HIS NAME?" shouted the girl.

"Whose name, my dear?" asked the puzzled miller.

"THE LITTLE MAN, you old toad!" snapped the girl.

"Oh no," said the miller, "he didn't." The poor girl began to despair and a big tear ran down her cheek and into her boiled egg.

"Don't cry," said her father, "I can tell you his name – it was painted on the side of his caravan: Rumply Crumply Stinky Pin. Magician. (Spaghetti Vests a Speciality)."

"That's it," cried the girl clapping her hands with joy.

That night, as she was feeding her guinea pig, the little man appeared again.

"Come on kid, have you given up yet? Don't waste your time, just hand me the pet."

"I'll just try again," said the clever girl. "I might be lucky this time. Is it Benny Badger-Brain or Eddy Earwax-Eater?"

The little man rolled with laughter.

"Perhaps it's Trevor Telephone Bone Helicopter-Head!"

The little man was lying on the bed, kicking his legs in the air.

"I'll have one last try," said the miller's daughter, "and the guinea pig is yours. Is it…RUMPLY CRUMPLY STINKY PIN?"

The little man almost choked with rage and vanished in a clap of thunder, filling the air with a strange smell of burning spaghetti and old fish.

So, the miller's daughter lived happily ever after with her guinea pig and her old father, who hardly ever told lies any more.

"What will you call your little pet?" asked Eyebrow Snailsocks one day. "How about Guinea-Winnie-Winkie-Wigs or Pinkie-Poky-Porky-Piggy Pants?"

"Oh no, Daddy," said the girl. "I think I'll just call him…Fred."

"That is a very silly name," said Eyebrow Snailsocks. And it was.

The End

Daft Jack
and the
Bean
Stack

The throne shook like a rocking chair,
"Stop, oh Fool, it isn't fair!"
But the Fool would not turn back,
"And now this tale, it's called DAFT JACK..."

Daft Jack and his mother were so poor...
they lived under a cow in a field. His
mum slept at the front end...
and Jack slept at the udder end.

Daisy was a good cow, but the
problem was, Jack's mum was
fed up with milk. It was all
they ever had –

hot milk,

cold milk,

warm milk,

milk on toast,

milk pudding.

And on Sundays, for a special
treat, they had Milk Surprise
(which was really just milk
with milk on top).

Milk, milk
milky, milk!

59

Jack didn't mind milk, but his mother would have given anything for a change.

"I'M SICK AND TIRED OF MILK!" she would shout. "If I never taste another drop as long as I live it will be too soon. If only you were a clever boy, Jack, you would think of something."

"I have thought of something," said Jack. "It's a new kind of milkshake – it's milk flavoured."

Jack's mum chased him all around the field.

One day, a terrible thing happened; Jack was sitting in the field eating a Mini Milk lolly and his mum was having her after-milk rest when Daisy suddenly looked up at the grey sky, decided it was going to rain and, as all cows do, lay down.

"Right! That is it. I've had enough!" spluttered Jack's mum when Jack had pulled her out by the ankles. "You will have to take Daisy into town and sell her. But make sure you get a good price or I'll chase you around the field for a week."

Daft Jack was very sad because Daisy was more like a friend than just a roof over his head.

But he always liked to please his mother.
He made himself a milk sandwich for the
journey and Jack and Daisy set off towards the
town. It was a long way so they took it in
turns to carry each other.

Then at the top of a hill, they
met an old man sitting on a tree
stump with a shopping bag.
"That's a fine cow you're carrying,"
he said. "What's your name, sonny?"

"It's Jack," said Jack, "but everyone calls
me 'Daft', I don't know why."

"Well, Jack," said the old man.
"I'd like to buy that cow from you."

"I would like to sell this cow
too," said Jack, "but you'll
have to give me a good price
for her. Otherwise my
mum will chase me around
the field for a week."

"I can see you're a clever boy,"
said the old man, "and I'm in a good
mood today. So guess what I'm going to give you for that cow?"

"What?" said Jack.

The old man reached into his shopping bag.

"Beans!" said the old man. "Not just one bean! Not just two beans! I'm going to give you A WHOLE TIN OF BAKED BEANS."

Jack couldn't believe his luck. Not one bean, not two beans, but a WHOLE TIN of baked beans for just one old cow. It must have been his lucky day. At last his mum would be proud of him.

So Jack kissed Daisy goodbye and set off home carrying the tin of beans as carefully as he would carry a new born baby, feeling very pleased with himself.

As soon as he saw the field he began to shout, "Look Mum! All our troubles are over. Guess what I got for Daisy? Not one bean. Not two beans. But A WHOLE TIN COMPLETELY FULL OF BEANS! Why, Mother there must be A HUNDRED yummy beans in this tin, I knew you'd be pleased."

At the end of the week, when his mum had finished chasing him, Daft Jack and his mum sat down in the middle of the field.

"Oh, Jack," wailed his mum. "Now we haven't even got a cow to sleep under. If only you were a clever boy, you'd think of something."

"I have thought of something, Mum," said Jack. "Let's eat the beans."

So Daft Jack and his mum ate the beans. Then they had nothing left at all.

That night, Jack couldn't sleep. I can't do anything right, he thought sadly. My poor mother would be better off without me. I think I will run away into the big wide world and seek my fortune.

So Jack decided to leave a note for his mother. He couldn't find any paper so he tore the label from the bean tin. But there was something already written on the back of the baked bean label.

Jack held the paper up to the moonlight and read aloud…

"Congratulations! You have bought THE LUCKY BEAN TIN and won a FANTASTIC PRIZE for you and your family!"

Jack woke his mother. When she saw the message on the bean tin, she couldn't believe her eyes. "Oh Jack," she cried. "At last we will be able to buy a proper house."

"Yes," said Jack, "and I will buy poor Daisy back. I fancy a nice glass of milk."

And Jack's mum was too happy to chase him around the field.

In the morning they sent off the lucky bean label and soon their prize arrived – A WHOLE LORRY LOAD OF BAKED BEANS.

Jack and his mum didn't know what to say. They began to stack the tins in one corner of the field, but before they had finished a second lorry load of beans arrived.

And all day long the lorries kept coming.

By the evening there was a huge pile of bean tins. A STACK of bean tins. A COLOSSAL GLEAMING MONUMENTAL MOUNTAIN of bean tins. There were bean tins right up to the clouds.

So from that day Daft Jack and his mum ate beans. It was all they ever had –

hot beans,

cold beans,

warm beans,

beans on toast,

bean pudding.

And on Sundays, for a special treat, they had Bean Surprise (which was really just beans with beans on top).

Beans, beans, beansy beans!

Jack's mum would have given anything for a change.

"I'm SICK AND TIRED OF BEANS!" she shouted one day. "If I never eat another bean as long as I live it will be too soon. If only you were a clever boy, Jack, you would think of something."

"I have thought of something," said Jack. "Bean juice milkshake."

There wasn't room to chase Jack around the field because the bean stack was too big. So Jack's mum chased him up the bean stack instead.

Higher and higher, Jack hopped from tin to tin with his mum puffing and panting behind.

Until at last Jack climbed so high he left his mum far behind. But Jack didn't stop. He kept on climbing. He looked down at the world below. He saw the field as small as a handkerchief and his mum as tiny as an ant. And still Jack climbed higher.

When he was almost too tired to climb any more, Jack reached the top of the bean stack, way up in the clouds.

Jack looked around. To his amazement he saw an enormous castle with its great door wide open.

He tiptoed inside. It was the most incredible place he had ever seen.

Jack wandered from room to room. He found massive bedrooms with carpets as thick as snow drifts, a solar heated Jacuzzi, a living room with great armchairs and a TV screen the size of a cinema.

At last, Jack wandered into a wonderful kitchen fitted with every kind of gadget. Jack was interested in cooking and he climbed up to look at the giant sized microwave. Suddenly, the whole castle began to shake. A great voice roared.

"Fee, fi, fo, fum,

I've got a giant pain in my tum!"

Jack looked around in alarm and saw an enormous giant sitting at a table, rubbing his stomach and looking very miserable.

"'S not fair!" complained the giant. "All I ever get to eat is CHILDREN! And now I've got a belly ache…

Hot kids,

    cold kids,

        warm kids,

            kids on toast,

                kid pudding.

And on Sundays, for a special treat, I have Kid Surprise (but that's just kids with kids on top). I'd give ANYTHING for a change. I'M SICK AND TIRED OF KIDS! If I never ate another kid as long as I live it would be too soon…" He looked down at Jack.

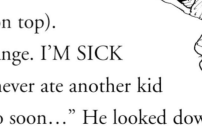

"AND NOW I'VE GOT TO EAT YOU TOO! 'S NOT FAIR!"

The giant reached out a huge hairy hand and grabbed Jack around the waist.

He lifted Jack kicking and struggling into the air and opened his vast black cave-like mouth with a tongue like a huge purple carpet.

Well, thought Jack, this is the end of Daft Jack and no mistake.

He was just about to be crunched into a million tiny daft pieces, when suddenly he had an idea.

"Er, excuse me, Mr Giant," he whispered nervously. "If you eat me it will only make your tummy ache worse. I can think of something much nicer. I don't suppose you like… beans, do you?"

"BEANS!" roared the giant "DO I LIKE BEANS? I YUMMY YUMMY LOVE 'em!"

So Jack took the giant by the hand and led him down the bean stack. And on the way, the giant told Jack how lonely he was, all by himself in the great big castle in the clouds with nothing to do but eat people.

Jack began to feel very sorry for the poor giant and took him home to meet his mum.

"Oh Jack," she cried. "Where ever have you bean?"

Jack's mum was very pleased to see Jack in one piece. But when she saw the giant…!

And when the giant saw Jack's mum…!

It was love at first sight.

"Fee, fi, fo, fum,
I'm going to marry
Daft Jack's mum!"

"Of course you are, dear," said Jack's mum, "but first you must be hungry after your long journey."

The giant looked at the bean stack, gleaming in the evening light as he licked his giant lips.

He began munching the beans. Not one tin, not two tins, but the whole stack of beans. And he didn't even stop to open the tins.

So Daft Jack's mum married the giant, and they were very happy. They all went to live in the giant's wonderful castle in the sky.

Daft Jack opened a cafe in the giant's kitchen and he called it 'DAFT JACK'S SKY SNACKS'. And people came from far and wide and Jack grew rich and happy.

He served everything you can think of except milk…and beans!

The End

Snow White and the Seven Aliens

At that the King began to roar
And bang his fists upon the floor,
As yet another story comes
Of sweet SNOW WHITE and seven chums...

Snow White dreamed of becoming a pop star. She wanted to be number one in the charts, just like her hero, Hank Hunk from Boysnog.

Snow White had a beautiful voice. She was a great dancer too. And she could even write her own songs. Only one thing stood in her way – her wicked stepmother.

Once upon a time Snow White's stepmother had been a famous pop star. She had been the Mean Queen, lead singer in The Wonderful Wicked Witches. But now her voice was croaky and she was no longer a star. She had become mad with jealousy of Snow White.

"You will never be famous like me!" she would hiss. "You look too… ordinary. You don't even have a band. And besides, your nose is too small."

Then, the Mean Queen would storm out of the room, leaving poor Snow White to weep under the Boysnog posters in her bedroom.

Snow White's father was a kind little man. He liked doing jigsaw puzzles and making small Plasticine models. Although he loved his daughter, he was not strong enough to stand up to his wife.

The Mean Queen had a huge dressing-room at the top of the house, with dozens of mirrors and shelves of make-up, as if she were still a great star.

And sometimes she forced her poor husband to sit behind the dressing-table mirror and tell her that she was still beautiful…

"Mirror, Mirror, on the wall,
Who has the cutest nose of all?"

From behind the mirror, her terrified husband would reply…

"Mean Queen, you look a treat,
With a nose as perfect as a boiled sweet."

Then the Mean Queen would scream with laughter and march around the house croaking her ancient songs and remembering the day when The Wonderful Wicked Witches had appeared on the Christmas edition of *Top of the Pops*.

Now, Snow White often sat in the garden surrounded by little birdies and bunny rabbits, singing quietly in her beautiful clear voice. When she looked down, the Mean Queen would almost choke with rage.

Day by day, the Mean Queen could see that Snow White was growing into a very beautiful young woman. With that tiny pink nose…how the Mean Queen hated her.

Only the mirror brought her comfort…

"Mirror, Mirror, tell me true,
Is my nose as long as a didgeridoo?
That girl's nose is microscopic.
What are your feelings on this topic?"
And the mirror would reply…
"If you push me, I must admit,
Snow White's nose is a decent fit.
But your nose, oh Queen is really small,
In fact, it's hardly there at all."
And so it went on. Until, one terrible night, Snow White's father could stand the lies no longer. The Mean Queen demanded…

"Mirror, mirror, above the sink,
Tell me what you REALLY think,
It's time you started coming clean,
CHOOSE SNOW WHITE...OR ME, YOUR QUEEN!"

In a tiny, trembling voice, the mirror replied…

"All right. I've really had enough,
I'm fed up with the lies and stuff,
You are past it, old and sad,
Crinkly, wrinkly - really bad,
Your nose is sort of long and hairy,
Beside you, Snow White is a
Christmas fairy!"

The Mean Queen leapt to her feet. With a sweep of her bony hand, she sent her make-up and bottles of perfume crashing to the floor. She seized her husband by his collar, and lifted him off his feet.

"Get Snow White OUT OF MY HOUSE," she spat into his terrified face. "Make sure she NEVER EVER returns." The poor man crawled towards the door. But the Mean Queen had one more order – something so terrible that her husband quaked in his sandals… ☞

To prove that Snow White has really gone... BRING ME THAT TINY SNUBBY NOSE ON A COCKTAIL STICK!!!

And so, Snow White's father led his beautiful daughter far into the wild and dangerous city. With tears streaming down his face, he bought her an all-day bus pass and kissed his sweet daughter goodbye. Of course, he could not bring himself to cut off that precious snubby nose,

so he quickly modelled a false one out of some pink Plasticine which he always carried in his pocket. This he brought back to the Mean Queen on a cocktail stick.

When the Mean Queen saw the little nose, she screamed with laughter all over again. Then she did something so ghastly that her husband felt quite ill.

She took the Plasticine nose, dipped it in mayonnaise and ATE IT, served with a side salad and French fries.

"Mmm!!" she said licking her lips, "tasty!"

Meanwhile, poor Snow White wandered through the city, lost and alone.

It grew dark, and she started to feel afraid. Then, in the distance, she saw a dim green light between the buildings. Faint with hunger, she stumbled towards it and found herself in a clearing by a car park.

There in front of her was…a gleaming silver spacecraft!

A little ladder led up to a door where a flashing neon sign said: SWINGING SPACESHIP NIGHT CLUB.

Under this was pinned another smaller notice. This one read:

Cleaner wanted.

Apply within.

Too tired to feel afraid, Snow White pushed the bell.

Quietly, the door slid open and she stepped nervously inside.

And so it was that Snow White began her new life as a cleaner at the Swinging Spaceship Night Club. The hours were long, the

pay was poor, but at least some good bands played from time to time. "Who knows?" sighed Snow White, "perhaps I might even hear Hank Hunk from Boysnog one day!"

One evening, Snow White was told to prepare the dressing-room for a special band who would be playing that night.

In the dressing-room she found seven identical chairs. Laid neatly on the seven identical chairs were seven identical space helmets. I wonder who will be changing in here? she thought.

Just then, she heard strange voices singing outside in the corridor…

"Hi ho, hi ho, it's off to space we go…"

What an awful song, thought Snow White. I wonder who wrote those terrible lyrics? The door opened and in stepped seven of the most extraordinary creatures Snow White had ever seen.

"Hi," said the first stranger. "We are the Seven Aliens. We are booked to perform tonight. We are number 4,324 in the pop charts, you know. Meet the band…"

"And what about you?" laughed Snow White, pointing at the very funny looking alien who had spoken to her first. "What is your name?"

"He's BOTTY!!" shouted all the other aliens together.

"Well," giggled Snow White. "I am very pleased to meet you. Now, if you like, I will polish your space helmets before you go on stage."

While Snow White polished, she sang a sad and beautiful song. The Seven Aliens were entranced.

"That was wonderful," gurgled Grotty, when she had finished. "Tell us your name."

"I am Snow White," said Snow White.

"Oh, Snow White," sniffed Snotty, "the truth is, we cannot sing for toffee and the only words we can write are 'hi ho, hi ho'. If you would join our band, we would blast up the charts like a rocket into space."

And so it was that Snow White and the Seven Aliens played their very first gig at the Swinging Spaceship Night Club.

Meanwhile, at home, Snow White's father wept over his lost daughter until his jigsaw puzzles were soggy. The Mean Queen, on the other hand, was in a very good mood. She went to admire herself in her magic mirror…

"Mirror, mirror, spill the beans,
Am I now the queen of queens?
Now Snow White's nose is in my tummy,
You must admit I look quite yummy."

But to her horror the mirror replied…

"I don't want to shock you, rotten Queen,

But that nose was made of Plasticine,
Snow White's nose is on her face,
She's with some blokes from
outer space."

The Mean Queen turned purple.
She smashed the mirror into a
thousand jagged pieces.

Back at the Swinging Spaceship Night Club, Snow White and the Seven Aliens had been a huge success. A record producer had heard them play and signed them on the spot.

Snow White's dream was coming true. As Christmas approached, her single 'Snow White Alien Rap' crept higher and higher up the charts, eventually even overtaking Hank Hunk and Boysnog.

Snow White and the Seven Aliens were booked to appear on the Christmas edition of *Top of the Pops*.

Snow White was terribly nervous. She was sure the Mean Queen would do something to spoil her good fortune. The aliens made her promise to lock her dressing-room door and not let anyone in but them.

But with only half an hour to go before the programme, someone rattled the door handle, and a voice called…

"Snow White, Snow White, the door is stuck,
It is Hank Hunk here to wish you luck."

Snow White thought the voice sounded a little strange, but she just had to see if it was really Hank Hunk from Boysnog come to see her!

She opened the door a tiny crack. In burst a tall figure with blond hair. It looked like Hank Hunk…but surely there was something strange about his nose?

"So you're a pop star now, Snow White,
But you will surely faint with fright.
Your band are weird, your song is crummy,
You'll freeze on stage like a plastic dummy.
The world will watch you on TV,
But you'll never be as good as ME!
Ah, ha hah haar!!"

Alas! It was the Mean Queen. When the aliens came to collect Snow White they found her completely frozen with stage fright.

No matter how they tried to reassure her, Snow White simply could not move her arms and legs, let alone dance or sing. In despair, they carried her, like a statue, out of the dressing-room and laid her gently on the stage.

"It's no use," bawled Botty. "We'll have to sing 'hi ho, hi ho…'"

The programme started.

"FAN-TABULOUS Christmas Greetings, pop fans," called the announcer. "We've got a SEN-SATIONAL seasonal line up for you, including the incredible new discovery, Snow White and those Seven EXTREMELY STRANGE Aliens. We've also got Hank Hunk and Boysnog and later…"

Snow White was still unable to move. To the Seven Aliens, it seemed like a hundred years passed by. Then, at the back of the studio, someone began to push his way through the crowd.

"Let me through," he said, "I'm a qualified heart-throb. I simply must see her."

It was Hank Hunk! This time it really was him. Snow White's heart began to flutter.

"Oh Snow White," whispered Hank, "please sing. Sing for me."

He bent towards Snow White. A long blond curl
fell across one eye. Gently he kissed her lips.

Snow White leapt to her feet.

"OK BOYS. Let's GROO-VE!!" she shouted.

Snow White and the Seven Aliens leapt into
the spotlight and began to play. Across the
nation, every family threw down their Christmas crackers and
began gyrating to the fantastic sounds on TV.

Everybody, except one person. High in her dark dressing-room,
the Mean Queen stared into her shattered mirror and muttered…

"Mirror, mirror, smashed to bits,
Today I really feel…the PITS!"

But her husband, jiving in front of the TV,
called up to her…

"That's funny, honey, I feel quite perky,
Come downstairs and have some turkey,
If you're good, you never know
I might get out the mistletoe."

On New Year's Eve, there
were seven special guests at
Hank and Snow White's wedding. Their names were
Scotty, Spotty, Dotty, Snotty, Potty, Grotty and Botty.

And they all blasted off for a honeymoon in the stars.

"Hi ho, hi ho…"

The End

The Emperor's Underwear

"That tale, oh Fool, was far too weird.
You've made me dribble in my beard."
The Fool thinks of the crown he'll share,
Begins THE EMPEROR'S UNDERWEAR...

There was once a country where no one wore any clothes at all.

It was a very sensible thing to do. There was no washing, no ironing, no mending, no folding, no putting away, no dressing and undressing.

So there was plenty of time for really important things, like climbing trees and doing handstands and dancing about in the sunshine.

All through the summer it was the happiest country in the world.

Without their clothes, everyone was treated alike – big or small, rich or poor.

Even the Emperor was just like an ordinary person, without a crown or fancy clothes.

In fact people spent most of the day laughing out loud, because everything seemed so funny.

After all, even strict headmasters aren't very frightening in their birthday suits.

Of course, there were no uniforms either. So when the police chased the robbers it was hard to tell one from the other. They all got into such a muddle that they just fell about laughing.

There was no doubt about it – in summer, it was the happiest country in the world. But in winter…that was a different story all together. All through the winter, the icy north wind whistled around the streets until every bare botty turned blue with cold.

One particularly chilly morning, the Emperor woke up with goose pimples all over his royal body. The wind moaned around the palace, and the Emperor moaned around the palace, too.

He jumped up and down and rubbed his hands together, but by breakfast time even his goose pimples had goose pimples.

All morning the snow fell, and throughout the land people stayed indoors and shivered like blueberry jellies.

Then, at lunch time, there was a knock at the palace door. In came two strange men.

The Emperor could see straight away that they had come from a different country because they were wearing CLOTHES! But being a kind Emperor, he tried not to laugh.

"Good day, Your Noble Nakedness," said the first man, stamping the snow from his boots.

"Greetings, Oh Royal Rudeness," said the second man, brushing the ice from his woollen hat.

"We are tailors from a distant nation," they said.

The Emperor wasn't sure what a tailor was, but he smiled and shivered politely.

"We have come to make you the most beautiful bloomers in the world to keep your royal bottom warm," they announced.

"What?" said the Emperor. "Me? Wear knickers? You must be joking. I have to set an example to my people, you know."

"Yes, yes, Your Beautiful Bareness, but these are not ordinary pantaloons, they are MAGIC KNICKERBOCKERS, because they will be completely INVISIBLE to the naked eye (if you'll pardon the pun).

No one will be able to see them at all – unless they are a complete banana brain, that is!"

"Amazing!" said the Emperor, his teeth chattering a bit more.

"Mind you," continued the tailors, "magic undies don't come cheap. You will have to start us an Underwear Account at the bank so that we can buy all the magic wool we need."

So the tailors moved into the palace. Night and day, and day and night, they cut and stitched and sewed and made, not one pair of underwear, but hundreds and thousands of pairs of every shape and size.

There were Y-fronts and Y-Not Fronts, and Boxer Shorts and Thermal Long-Johns and Purple Posing Pouches and Itsy Bitsy Teeny Weeny Yellow Polka Dot Bikinis and Woolly Winter Warmers and even Leopard Skin Tonga Thongs.

Of course, the Emperor and everyone at the palace could see *exactly* what they were doing, but no one said a word in case people thought that *they* were complete banana brains.

At last the tailors brought the Emperor a pair of Y-Fronts and a woolly vest, all extra large size.

The Emperor allowed the tailors to help him squeeze into them.

"Oooh!" he said, "they're all nice and warm – even though I can't see them!"

The Emperor was so pleased with his new underwear, he hopped on to his bicycle and went for a ride around the town.

When he had gone, the tailors began to laugh and rub their wicked hands together, "Snee hee heee!"

The Emperor rode proudly backwards and forwards along the High Street and although it was still snowing, a large crowd gathered to watch.

Of course, everyone could see the royal underwear perfectly well, but they didn't want anyone to think that *they* were silly old banana brains, so they said nothing at all; only clapped and cheered as the Emperor pedalled by.

All of a sudden, a tiny boy who was shivering on his father's shoulders pointed his little cold finger at the Emperor and shouted, "Dat man wearing panties!"

"Shh!" hissed his father. "That's the Emperor, and he's not wearing anything!"

"Oh yes, he is!" shouted the boy. "Dat man wearing nice warm woolly panties. Me want some woolly panties too!"

"The Emperor is wearing panties," someone whispered. "The Emperor's wearing underwear!"

"Yes!" everyone shouted. "The Emperor's wearing underwear and WE WANT SOME TOO!"

The Emperor turned all red inside his woollies and pedalled back to the palace.

"I really am a big banana brain," he sighed. "Whatever have I started?"

In no time at all, the wicked tailors opened a big underwear shop in the High Street and people soon began queuing outside.

It wasn't long before everyone started wearing underwear. Some people wore socks too, and trousers and shirts, and even ties on Sundays.

And of course, it wasn't long before they had to spend all their time washing…

…and ironing…

…and putting away.

Although the people weren't cold anymore, they didn't laugh quite so often. Policemen looked like policemen, teachers looked like teachers…and the Emperor looked so important in his royal clothes that nobody spoke to him anymore. He began to feel very lonely and fed up.

One hot day, in the middle of summer, when everyone was sweltering in their woollen clothes, the Emperor decided he had had enough.

He pulled off his royal robes and his crown and hopped back on to his bicycle. Then he rode proudly up and down the High Street carrying a large sign. It said…
DARE TO BE BARE.
And on the back it said…
IT AIN'T RUDE TO BE NUDE.

All the people turned out to clap and cheer. Then they began to pull off their clothes too!

The wicked tailors sat in their shop and got hotter and hotter and more miserable. No one was interested in buying anything.

In no time at all everyone was laughing again – just as they had before.

Soon even the tailors joined in. They set up a stall selling suntan lotion and ice lollies instead.

But the person who laughed loudest of all was the Emperor himself.

"Perhaps I am a banana brain," he chuckled. "But I'm a big, bare, happy, old banana brain!"

And he cycled away into the sunshine.

The End

The
Fried
Piper of
Hamstring

"That story really was the worst,
I thought I'd laugh until I burst,
I'm happy, Fool, to share my crown.
Spare me the tale of HAMSTRING TOWN..."

The grown ups in Hamstring Town were the bossiest people in the ENTIRE UNIVERSE. They would never leave their kids alone…"Nag nag nag." "Do this." "Don't do that." "Wash your hair." "Eat your greens." "Go to sleep." It never ever stopped. The grown ups had rules for everything. Every child had to know them by heart…

"NO TOYS. NO TV. NO TREATS.
NO SINGING. NO SWINGING. NO SWEETS.
NO PARTIES. NO PRESENTS. NO PETS.
NO BURPING. NO BIRTHDAYS. NO BETS.
NO SKIPPING. NO SPITTING. NO SUN.
NO FOOTBALL. NO FRIED FOOD...
...NO FUN!"

The grown ups were especially strict about the fried food.

"All those greasy chips and hamburgers will give you spots and make you lazy," they would tell their little ones.

So the poor children of Hamstring were allowed only organic fruit and vegetables, three times a day, and NO snacks between meals.

Everything in Hamstring Town was spick and span. Little girls had shiny hair in pretty bows. Boys wore short trousers until their thirty-fifth birthday, even if their legs were hairy. In the evening, families had spelling tests together.

It was boring. It was gloomy. It was DULL!

But, of all the bossy grown ups in Hamstring Town, no one was stricter than the Mayor. The Mayor of Hamstring spent all his time inventing new rules to make things even tidier. He didn't like children and he especially hated animals.

"Animals are so messy," he would snarl. "Let's have a new law. From now on, all cows must be toilet trained. And BIRDS..." he shouted, "...birds are dirty little creatures. From today all birds must wear nappies."

The boys and girls of Hamstring would have given anything for their own little puppy or a baby hamster or even a stick insect, but pets were strictly forbidden in Hamstring Town.

As the days passed, things got worse and worse.

On Monday the Mayor banned music, moustaches and morris men.

On Tuesday he banned chewing gum, chocolate and chattering.

On Wednesday he banned watches, weeds and whispering.

On Thursday he banned theatres, thunderstorms and thinking.

On Friday he banned freckles, frogs and fireworks.

On Saturday he banned scratching, scarecrows and smiling.

On Sunday – well on Sunday some of the children sneaked off to meet secretly. "This has gone too far," whispered one of the big children.

"Soon there will be nothing left to ban. We must do something NOW. We must stop that mad Mayor."

"We need some help," said a little girl at the back.

"Yes," said a boy. "We need a person who isn't afraid of grown ups."

So the children typed out a secret message. It said:

S.O.S.

Hamstring kids urgently require

A FEARLESS HERO

to save the town from a power mad mayor

and too many RULES!

HELP! Come quick.

The children sent the message out to every newspaper in the land. They sent it by e-mail. They faxed it. They sent it out on the Internet.

Replies to: http://www rulebuster.@hamstring/co.

Then they went home for tea.

At first light, as the children wandered wearily to school, they spotted a strange figure high on a mountain top above the town.

The children could tell straight away that the stranger was not from their town because he was dressed in the most extraordinary way! Instead of grey shorts, he wore red and yellow jeans and a bomber jacket to match. His hair was tied in a ponytail; a gleaming silver saxophone hung round his neck. Most outrageous of all, the boy was sitting on a dazzling mountain bike.

To the children's amazement, the stranger leapt on to the saddle and hurtled down the hillside to where they were standing.

In a great cloud of dust, the bike spun to a halt.

It was only then that the children realised the stranger was holding something in his gloved hands…something terrible… something so wicked, it was banned through-out all Hamstring…a Mega-Burger with French fries, all sprinkled with salt and dripping with tomato ketchup!

A gasp ran through the crowd. The children stared wide-eyed as the boy began to speak in strange musical words:

"I was out on my bike, just takin' a cruise,
I nearly freaked out when I heard the news.
Said, 'I'll hit the road and burn on down,
To help those dudes in Hamstring Town.'
Yeah, I'm the Fried Piper and I am hip,
Any of you cool cats care for…A CHIP?"

The children of Hamstring stood frozen. They couldn't believe their eyes.

Then, very slowly, a tiny boy stepped forward. He looked around, and, quick as a flash, he grabbed a chip from the Fried Piper's outstretched hand and stuffed it into his mouth. It was the first chip he had ever eaten. And it was DELICIOUS!

In a second, everyone had gathered round, stuffing chips into their mouths, laughing and chattering and admiring the beautiful bike.

"But…but are you really allowed a bike?" someone asked. "What about the Rules?"

The Fried Piper only laughed and tossed back his golden hair,

"You know, rules ain't cool. I do what I like,
I dig fried food and I LOVE my bike.
If you follow me, then pretty soon,
You'll hear me blowin' a RADICAL tune!"

The children knew they should be at school, but somehow, they couldn't help it. They *had* to follow that wonderful smell of fried chips and tomato sauce. The Fried Piper led them slowly down the road towards the centre of Hamstring Town.

that moment, the wicked Mayor was searching for children who were late for school. Suddenly he heard an unusual noise. It sounded like scurrying feet. It sounded like chattering. It sounded like laughing. It sounded like…CHILDREN!

The Mayor spun around.

"ARE YOU MAD?" he shouted, "This is SCHOOL TIME. Have you forgotten Rule 48B, Subsection 19? It clearly says that any child absent from school for any reason shall…"

The Mayor stopped. He stared. His jaw hung open. The Fried Piper stepped out of the crowd. He pushed his bike into the town square, where the sun cast long shadows…

"HEY! You Mayor. You big fat dude,
We don't dig your rules, we don't dig your food.
You got too much belly and not enough hair,
You're what I call a real NIGHT MAYOR!"

The children began to laugh. They just couldn't stop.

The Mayor struggled for something to say. He turned red. The children laughed more.

At last the Mayor blurted out,

"THIS…THIS IS AN OUTRAGE! Where are your shorts, young man? There are rules…RULES…RULES!!"

Slowly the Fried Piper stepped forward. He leaned his bike carefully against a railing. His long fingers drummed on his saxophone. His dark eyes fixed on the Mayor. A strange silence fell over the town. In a firm, low voice the stranger whispered, "Chill out, Mayor. That's enough of your threats, Us kids need fun and we need... PETS!"

At the sound of the word 'pets', the Mayor gasped.

The Piper put his gleaming silver instrument to his lips and began to play – a weird haunting tune which rose up above the houses and all across the mountains around Hamstring Town.

Everyone stood in silence, until they heard a faint, distant squeaking. To the Mayor's horror, a tiny baby rat came scampering along the main street, sniffing the air and twitching its little whiskers. The rat was followed by a guinea pig. The guinea pig by a hamster. Behind the hamster bounced two long-eared rabbits. The rabbits were followed by kittens. The kittens by puppies. And still the Piper played on.

The children of Hamstring scooped up the little animals and started to stroke and kiss them.

The Mayor began to shake. "The Rules," he croaked. "The Rules…" But the Fried Piper didn't miss a note.

More and more pets came hopping and bounding into the main square of Hamstring. Big and small. Tortoises, budgies, ponies. Parrots, dogs, cats. Squeaking, yapping, barking. Whistling, grunting, yelping.

The children were delighted. They ran to meet the new animals who jumped up and licked their happy faces. Behind the noise, the strange tune continued.

Donkeys, goats, monkeys. Lizards, lambs, frogs. Rolling, running, racing. Scurrying, scampering, chasing.

A large dog licked the Mayor's ear. A monkey climbed on to his hat. The Mayor put his hands to his face and started to weep. "The Rules," he sobbed. "Oh, the Rules…"

The bossy grown ups of Hamstring had been watching their children in dismay. Now they turned and ran. Down the street and out of the town. Over the mountains and far far away.

Only one person could not keep up. The Mayor ran as fast as his fat little legs would carry him, but as he reached the edge of the mountains, a huge kangaroo bounded after him. She scooped him up and shoved him into her pouch. As they bounced back to town, the Mayor squealed, "NO KANGAROOS! NO HOPPING! NO BOUNCING!"

That evening, there was great feasting in Hamstring. The children lit a fire in the town square and the Mayor was made to cook the most enormous fry-up of all time: fried eggs, fried bread, fried bananas and – most of all – hundreds and thousands of chips, dripping in tomato sauce. Late into the night, the children and their pets danced to the wild tunes of the Fried Piper.

The party lasted four long days. When it was over, the grown ups crept quietly home from their hiding places in the mountains.

The Mayor was still busy cleaning the frying pan so the Fried Piper had made one or two rules of his own.

"Gather round dudes, here's my number one rule:
Think for yourself and you'll always be cool.
Like what you do and do what you like,
Hey! Anyone seen my mountain bike?"

And the Fried Piper rode away into the sunset.

To this very day there are no rules in Hamstring town. The people do exactly what they please. They are the coolest cats for miles around. And the hippest, smoothest, most radical dude of them all is…that crazy old Mayor himself.

Yeah!

The End

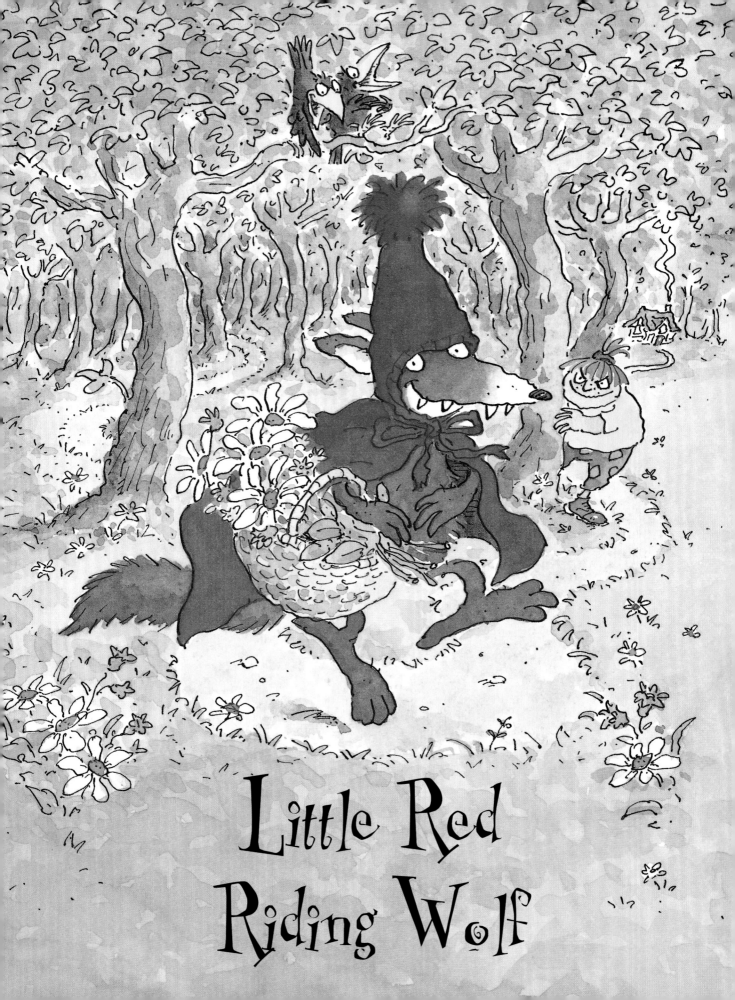

Little Red Riding Wolf

The King lay rolling on the floor,
"I BEG YOU, FOOL, NO MORE, NO MORE!"
Too late - the final tale's begun,
With RIDING WOLF the Fool has won.

In the very darkest corner of the deep dark wood sat the Big Bad Girl.

The Big Bad Girl was just about as BIG and BAD as a girl can be, and all the woodland animals were afraid of her.

She hung about beside the forest path and carved her name on trees. She shouted rude things at any little animal who passed by: "Come on, Big Ears. Hop to it!"

The Big Bad Girl tripped up little deer. She stole fir cones from baby squirrels and threw them at the poor little hedgehogs. The woodland birds didn't dare to sing when the Big Bad Girl was around!

But the person the Big Bad Girl liked to tease most of all was a charming little wolf cub who often passed by on his way to visit his dear old granny wolf.

Little Wolfie was the sweetest, fluffiest, politest little cub you could ever hope to meet. He would run along the path, *skippety-skip*, carrying a basket of freshly baked goodies for Old Granny Wolf, singing all the time…

"I'm a little wolfie, good and sweet,
I am tidy, I am neat.
With a basket full of lovely grub,
I am Granny's favourite cub."

"Wot's in yer basket today, Little-Weedy-Wolfie-Wimp?" snarled the Big Bad Girl. "Mmmm, apple pies? I'll take those. Jam sandwiches? Very tasty."

"Oh dear, oh dear! Now there will be nothing for dear old Granny Wolf," wailed Little Wolfie. And his little wolfie tears rolled into the empty basket.

Now, the Big Bad Girl's father was not big and bad at all. He was a kind old hat-maker who loved hats in every shape and size, and thought everyone should wear one night and day. But the sad truth was, his hats were so awful that nobody would buy them. He had only sold one nightcap in his entire life, and the family was terribly poor.

"I can't understand it," he sighed. "I make these marvellous hats from dawn till dusk until my fingers are worn to the bone, but even my own daughter will not wear them. Please, my dear," he begged, "wear this one for me."

"Father," answered the appalling child, "I would rather wear one of your old socks on my head than this hat. Why can't you get a decent job? Nobody is a hat-maker these days. Couldn't you be a woodcutter like other people's dads?"

The Big Bad Girl hated hats so much that as soon as her father gave her a new one, she would run into the woods and give it to a baby badger or a little squirrel to wear, whether they liked it or not.

Then, to her father's dismay, she would return home, bareheaded, pretending she had lost the hat in the forest.

One day, however, the Big Bad Girl's father made her a hat that was more ridiculous than anything he had made before. This one was a real monster. It was bright red with a woolly bobble on top, little flaps over the ears and dangly bows to tie under the chin. It even had a small red cape to match. The old man was delighted with his creation. "Surely my daughter will LOVE this one," he laughed, jumping up and down with excitement.

But the Big Bad Girl said, "Father, you have made some vile things in your life, but this hat is THE PITS! I would rather wear your old underpants on my head. You have as much fashion sense as a dung-beetle!"

As her father lay weeping in his workshop, the Big Bad Girl stomped into the forest to find some unsuspecting little animal to wear the red riding hat. But, alas, this one was so awful that no one would touch it. Even the Woodland Oxfam shop sent her away.

The Big Bad Girl sat by the forest path wondering what to do. "Surely someone will be stupid enough to wear this hat," she said. As she spoke, she heard a delightful little song…

"I'm a little wolfie, smart and clean,
never nasty, never mean.
Hello flowers, hello trees,
Hello humble bumble bees."

And who should come along the path, *skippety-skip*, but Little Wolfie.

"Ah, ha!" sniggered the Big Bad Girl. "Here comes Creepy-Cutesy-Custard-Cub. My red riding hat would suit him perfectly! I will trick him into wearing it. Then I will make fun of him FOREVER! Heh heh heh!"

"Where are you going, Little Fluffy Flea Face?" growled the Big Bad Girl.

"I am off to visit my darling old granny wolf," replied Little Wolfie, politely.

"Well, I have just seen yer old granny wolf," lied the rotten girl. "You can't see her today because she is poorly and might give you her old granny wolf germs."

"Oh, poor old Granny Wolf," sighed Little Wolfie, sadly.

"But," continued the wicked girl, "she has made you a lovely sort of hat thing. She told me to give it to you and tell you never to take it off, night or day, even if people laugh at you."

Little Wolfie was very pleased…until he saw the revolting red riding hat. Then even he had doubts.

But being a good little chap and wanting to please his granny, he tied it on his fluffy little head with the dangly ribbons.

The Big Bad Girl almost choked with laughter. Holy Sweaty Snake Socks! she thought. This little wolf is UNBELIEVABLY stupid.

But Little Red Riding Wolf said 'thank you' politely and set off home, *skippety-skip*, chattering away to himself. "How pleased I am with my new riding hat that Granny has made me. From now on I will call myself *Little Red Riding Wolf.* That will please her even more."

The Big Bad Girl rolled on the path and roared with laughter. "Holy Newt's Knickers! LITTLE RED RIDING WOLF!! What a name! A wolf should be called *Hairy Howler* or *Bone Cruncher* or *Old Yellow Eyes*. Little Red Riding Wolf is a TERRIBLE name."

All that day, Little Wolfie wore the red riding hat and tried not to notice when people laughed at him. The next morning he said to himself, "Surely my dear old granny wolf will be better today. I will run along the path and show her how pleased I am with my lovely hat." And off he went, *skippety-skip*…

"I'm a little wolfie, so polite,
I am brave, I am bright.
I am happy, I am good,
In my new red riding hood."

BUT, by the side of the path, in the middle of the deep dark wood, blowing bubbles with her gum, something REALLY NASTY was waiting for him…

"Oi! Tomato Head!"

"I am not Tomato Head," said Little Red Riding Wolf, fighting back the tears. "I am Little Red Riding Wolf."

"Where are you going, Ketchup Cap?" demanded the Big Bad Girl, wiping her filthy nose on the back of her hand.

"I am going to dear old Granny Wolf's house to see if she is better and to thank her for this lovely hat. Now, excuse me while I fill my basket with these pretty spring flowers for her kitchen table."

While Little Red Riding Wolf picked his flowers, the Big Bad Girl picked her nose thoughtfully. "That wrinkly old Granny Wolf will spoil my fun," she said to herself. "I will take a shortcut to her house. If she gives me any trouble, I will lock her in the cupboard, then I will pretend that I am old Granny Wolf. I bet she is even smaller and weedier than little Strawberry Top."

So the Big Bad Girl ran as quickly as she could to old Granny Wolf's house. It was a very big house for a little old granny wolf.

But Granny Wolf was out chopping wood in the forest.

The Big Bad Girl climbed in the back window and ran indoors, just as Little Red Riding Wolf tapped at the door.

"Old Granny Wolf, old Granny Wolf. It is I, Little Red Riding Wolf in my brand new hat."

"Holy Hopping Hedgehog Droppings! That was quick," said the Big Bad Girl. She ran up the stairs and searched for somewhere to hide. She noticed a huge bed, but how could she make herself look like an old granny wolf?

On a hook on the back of the door, the Big Bad Girl found Granny Wolf's pink lacy nightcap. Little Wolfie had bought it for Granny Wolf's birthday, but she never really wore it. Of course, the Big Bad Girl HATED hats – and this one was even worse than the red riding hat.

But the Big Bad Girl had no choice. She pulled the ghastly nightcap right down to her eyes and climbed into the bed, just as Little Red Riding Wolf came running up the stairs, *skippety-skip.*

"Granny Wolf, Granny Wolf. Where are you?" he called.

"Er, over 'ere, Little Woolly Hood Head," answered the Big Bad Girl.

"Oh Granny Wolf, Granny Wolf, thank you for the beautiful hat you made me. Doesn't it look wonderful?"

"Er…yeah, Little Bobble Brain…really wicked," replied the Big Bad Girl.

"But Granny Wolf, Granny Wolf, what a tiny voice you have and what

small teeth you have too. Perhaps you are still poorly. You seem so pale and weedy today."

"Listen, Little Jam Man, you should learn not to make personal remarks!" snapped the Big Bad Girl.

"But Granny Wolf, Granny Wolf what small ears you have. In fact…I don't think you are my Granny Wolf at all. She is MUCH bigger than you."

At that precise moment Granny Wolf pushed open the door.

Granny Wolf was ENORMOUS. She had huge yellow eyes, big sharp teeth and a long dribbly tongue. She was carrying a great sharp axe.

"Ah, Little Wolfie," she said. "What a nice surprise. You are just in time for tea. But why are you wearing that ridiculous hat? And what is this thing in my bed? It looks like a Big Bad Girl – a very tasty Big Bad Girl – JUST RIGHT FOR MY BIG BAD TEA!"

The Big Bad Girl leapt out of bed, down the stairs, out of the door, into the forest and along the path as fast as her big bad legs would carry her. She hammered on her father's door.

"Father, Father," yelled the Big Bad Girl. "Let me in. Let me in. I will be good. I will do whatever you ask."

Her father peeped out of the window. He couldn't believe what he was seeing. There was his daughter wearing a delightful night cap. It reminded him of one he had made himself many years before. He remembered it well because it was the only one he had ever sold.

"I will let you in," he said. "But only if you promise to wear a hat night and day – the one you are wearing now suits you beautifully!"

And so from that day on, the Big Bad Girl became a Big Good Girl (for most of the time). She found a job as a woodcutter, and her boss kept a very careful, big yellow eye on her.

The Big Good Girl kept her promise to wear a hat every day, although it was usually a chainsaw helmet. And the red riding hat was useful when they had an especially long load.

The King lived happily ever after.
The palace echoed with his laughter,
Throughout the kingdom peace has grown,
And Serious and Silly share the throne.